TOMEK BOGACKI

Circus Girl

FRANCES FOSTER BOOKS

FARRAR STRAUS GIROUX

NEW YORK

It was late spring. I remember the day very well. Strange sounds coming from outside woke me earlier than usual. I jumped out of bed and ran to the window.

A colorful caravan of carriages was passing by. I spelled out the letters painted on the side—C-I-R-C-U-S.

The circus was coming to our town! I wanted to follow it, but I had to go to school.

That day we couldn't wait
for school to be over. Only
Tim didn't seem to be as
excited as the rest of us.
Tim was the smallest one in
the class and kept to himself.
He always went straight home
from school and never played
with us. No one paid any
attention to him.

The circus tent was going up in a big field on the outskirts of town. After school we all went to watch—all except Tim.

The next day our teacher brought a new girl to our classroom. She was tall and seemed a bit older.

"This is your new friend," said the teacher. "She will be with us while the circus is in town."

I am sure the teacher told us her name, but we just called her Circus Girl.

We all looked around, wondering where she would sit. There was only one seat that was not taken, and that was next to Tim. Circus Girl sat down beside him at the desk right behind me.

That day Circus Girl left school
in a hurry.
"See you at the parade," she said
as she walked out the door.

The whole town turned out for this
big event. Streets were filled with
clowns, magicians, and acrobats.
Finally we saw Circus Girl holding
a polka-dot umbrella and balancing
on a big elephant.

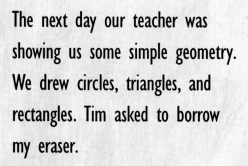

The next day our teacher was showing us some simple geometry. We drew circles, triangles, and rectangles. Tim asked to borrow my eraser.

"Can't you see I'm using it," I said abruptly.

Circus Girl gave me a strange look. I pretended I didn't see it and went back to my triangles. Then she asked to borrow my eraser. I turned around. She was smiling at me.

"Sure, here you go." I broke my eraser in two and handed half to her.

"Thank you," she said and then gave the eraser to Tim, who was as surprised as I was. After class she gave the eraser back to me.

The last class—drawing—was usually my favorite. But that day I didn't enjoy it. All I could think about was Circus Girl and Tim, and what had happened with the eraser. I turned around, and I saw Tim working on his drawing.

"I'm sorry," I said, and handed him half of my eraser. "You may keep it," I added.
"Thank you," said Tim with a smile. Circus Girl smiled, too.

That afternoon, as I left school, Circus Girl caught up with me on the stairs and invited me to go home with her to the circus grounds.

She showed me the caravan where she lived, and introduced me to all her friends. I was curious about everything, so she let me stay to watch the rehearsal.

On Saturday I went with my family to a real performance. Everything seemed magic. The musicians played, the clowns made everyone laugh, the lions did their tricks, but best of all was watching Circus Girl balancing on the back of a pony. I was so proud that she was my friend.

I went back to see her on Sunday. But she was busy getting ready for the midday performance and didn't have time for me.

I was sad and disappointed as I walked away, wondering what I would do for the rest of the day. Then I noticed Tim. Without thinking, I ran up to him.

We spent the whole afternoon together, and I was glad not to be alone.

On Monday the circus was closed, and the performers had the day off. But they still practiced their acts. This time Circus Girl invited both Tim and me to come after school and watch rehearsals.

She showed us her new act and what she most liked doing.

"What do you like?" she asked Tim, who, as usual, had been very quiet.
"The flying trapeze artists," answered Tim.
"No, I mean what do you like to do?" said Circus Girl.
"Oh!" said Tim. "I can show you. Both of you."

We followed Tim to his house and down a long hall to his room. There, hanging from the ceiling, were airplanes—beautifully painted models carved out of wood. They looked as if they were flying. Tim told us about each one. He wasn't the least bit shy anymore.

That whole week that the circus was in town, the three of us—Tim, me, and Circus Girl—spent as much time together as we could, after school and between circus performances. We went to Tim's house again and again to see his airplanes and help him build a new one.

And then came Friday. This was our last day together. On Saturday the circus was leaving for the next town.

That night, Circus Girl invited Tim and me backstage to watch the last circus performance. I knew it was time to say goodbye, but somehow I wasn't sad. Circus Girl was excited about going to a new town and a new school. And Tim and I were thinking about all the things we could now do together.

On Saturday morning we waved goodbye to Circus Girl. Then, as the circus caravan crossed the meadow on its way to the next town, Tim and I flew the new airplane we had made together.

I often think that if it had not been for Circus Girl I would never have had this great friend, Tim.

Copyright © 2001 by Tomek Bogacki
All rights reserved
Distributed in Canada by Douglas & McIntyre Ltd.
Color separations by Hong Kong Scanner Arts
Printed and bound in the United States of America by Berryville Graphics
Art direction and design by Monika Keano
First edition, 2001
1 3 5 7 9 10 8 6 4 2

Library of Congress Cataloging-in-Publication Data
Bogacki, Tomasz.
    Circus Girl / Tomek Bogacki.— 1st ed.
        p. cm.
    "Frances Foster books"
    Summary: When a new girl comes to school while the circus is in
town, she helps two classmates become friends.
    ISBN 0-374-31291-5
    [1. Circus—Fiction. 2. Friendship—Fiction.] I. Title.

PZ7.B6357825 Ci 2001
[E]—dc21

                                                            00-57849